BRUNO
the bravest man

ORCHARD BOOKS
96 Leonard Street, London EC2A 4RH
Orchard Books Australia
14 Mars Road, Lane Cove, NSW 2066

First published in Great Britain in 1998
First paperback publication 1999

A CIP catalogue record for this book is available from the British Library.
1 86039 696 8 (hardback)
1 86039 698 4 (paperback)
Printed in Great Britain

BRUNO
the bravest man

Laurence Anholt

Illustrated by Tony Ross

ORCHARD BOOKS

We are going to meet Bruno.
We are going to meet the one and only Bruno, the bravest man alive.

Every day is an adventure for Bruno.
On Monday, Bruno moves a mountain.

On Tuesday, Bruno ties ten thieves to a tree.

On Wednesday, Bruno wrestles with a whale.

On Thursday, Bruno flies through a thunderstorm.

On Friday, Bruno fights a fierce fire.

On Saturday, Bruno saves seven sailors sinking in the sea.

On Sunday, Bruno has a rest from being brave.

Bruno has a little daughter. Her name is Kate.

Bruno says, “Kate, I want you to learn how to be big and brave like me. You can come with me when I do brave things. And you can carry the bags.”

So Bruno and Kate go to the desert. They rescue a baby camel who is lost in the sand.

Bruno is brave. Kate carries the bags.

Bruno and Kate go to the North Pole. Bruno saves an eskimo from a dangerous polar bear.

Bruno is brave. Kate carries the bags.

Bruno climbs a tall tower. An old lady is stuck on the roof.

Bruno is brave. Kate carries
the bags.

One day, there is a knock at Bruno's door.

"Help! Help! My little boy has been stolen by robbers. They carried him away to the jungle!"

Bruno doesn't waste a moment.
"Quick Kate. Pack up the bags."

Bruno jumps on his motorbike.
Kate gets the goggles from
the bag.

They roar down the motorway
and arrive at the airport.
Kate takes the tickets out of
the bag.

They fly all morning high above the ocean.
Kate serves sandwiches out of the bag.

They come to the jungle, but the plane can’t land.
Kate pulls the parachutes out of the bag.

They float down gently, but the trees are thick.
Kate chooses a chainsaw from out of the bag.

They run to a river, but the bridge is broken.

Kate unrolls the rope from the
top of the bag.

They creep down a path, but a gorilla tries to stop them. Kate brings a banana out of the bag.

They come to the cave where the robbers are hiding.
Kate brings the boxing gloves out of the bag.

They run into the cave and chase away the robbers.

Kate lifts the little boy into
the bag.

They return through the jungle, back to the ocean.

Kate blows up the lifeboat from the bottom of the bag.

They sail through a storm,
through rain and snow.

Kate reaches for the raincoats inside the bag.

At last they land safely where the boy's family is waiting.
Kate lifts the little boy out of the bag.

Bruno is brave. Kate carries the bags.

They arrive back home, tired
but happy.
Kate keeps the door key in
the pocket of the bag.

Bruno goes upstairs. Bruno is sleepy.
Kate passes him his pyjamas from out of the bag. But…

In the middle of the night, when everyone is asleep, Bruno the bravest man begins to cry.

Quick Kate, quick Kate, bring me the bag.

Bruno is a brave man.
But Bruno is scared by just
ONE THING.

So Kate takes his teddy bear out of the bag.